Dr Jekyll
and
Mr Hyde

Robert Louis Stevenson

Simplified by D K Swan
Illustrated by Tudor Humphries

Addison Wesley Longman Limited,
Edinburgh Gate, Harlow,
Essex CM20 2JE, England
and Associated Companies throughout the world.

First published 1991
Ninth impression 1997

ISBN 0-582-01818-8

Set in 10/13 point Linotron 202 Versailles
Produced by Longman Asia Limited, Hong Kong.
GCC/09

Acknowledgements
The cover background is a wallpaper design called NUAGE,
courtesy of Osborne and Little plc.

Stage 3: 1300 word vocabulary
Please look under *New words* at the back of this book
for explanations of words outside this stage.

Contents

Introduction

Robert Louis Stevenson

Robert Louis Stevenson was born in Scotland in 1850. He was the son of an engineer, and he hoped to be an engineer himself. He began training, but his poor health prevented his continuing. Partly because of his health troubles – mainly tuberculosis – he spent a large part of his life outside Britain.

Partly, then, his travelling was for his health. But it was also partly for love of travel. That love took him on a tour by canoe of the rivers and canals of Belgium and France. His descriptions of that tour were collected in *An Inland Voyage* (1878). It was followed by *Travels with a Donkey in the Cevennes* (1879) in which he wrote:

> I travel not to go anywhere, but to go. I travel for travel's sake. The great affair is to move.

In the year in which that book came from the printer, Stevenson travelled to America, in great discomfort in an emigrant ship, and by train across the United States to San Francisco. He married in California, but he and his wife soon began to travel again. The success of *Treasure Island* (1883), completed in Switzerland, made it possible for them to travel widely in search of places that were good for his health. People already loved his travel books and poetry. *Treasure Island* was quite different, but readers – both children and grown-ups – loved it. It began as a story appearing, a part each month, in a boys' magazine. It was at first the story of Long John Silver, with the title *The Sea Cook*. It soon became the story of Jim Hawkins and his adventures – a story of pirates and treasure – that is still enjoyed today.

In France, Stevenson began the collection of poems *A Child's Garden of Verses* (1885) in which some of his most delightful poetry appeared. Here are some of the best-known lines from that collection:

> In winter I get up at night
> And dress by yellow candle-light.
> In summer, quite the other way –
> I have to go to bed by day.
> I have to go to bed and see
> The birds still hopping on the tree,
> Or hear the grown-up people's feet
> Still going past me in the street.

The Stevensons loved the islands of the southern Pacific Ocean, and his health seemed better there. Finally they settled in Samoa, and it was there that Robert Louis Stevenson wrote some of his finest poetry and some of his best stories. The stories include the first of Stevenson's historical novels: *Kidnapped* (1886), the story of David Balfour and Alan Breck and their escape across Scotland. It is set in the troubled times that followed the "rising" of 1745, when the Scottish clans fought for Charles Edward Stuart, "Bonny Prince Charlie".

Kidnapped was followed (but not immediately) by *Catriona* (1893). *Catriona* continued the story of David Balfour and told of more exciting adventures of David and Alan, and of David's love for Catriona Drummond.

In between the two stories about David Balfour, there came another surprising book, the mystery story, *The*

Strange Case of Dr Jekyll and Mr Hyde (called *Dr Jekyll and Mr Hyde* in this Longman Classics edition). It was a surprise, but it was also a success. It is still a success, and a number of films and television plays about Jekyll and Hyde show the interest people have today in Stevenson's idea.

Robert Louis Stevenson died in Samoa in 1894.

Dr Jekyll and Mr Hyde

This is a mystery story. It is not what we would call a "thriller" – a book that tells a story of crime so exciting that it frightens the reader. And Stevenson did not mean it to be a thriller, though that is what the films and television plays often make it.

It is not a detective story like Conan Doyle's stories of Sherlock Holmes. (The first of these appeared in 1887, one year later than Stevenson's book.) In a detective story we (and the detective) are usually trying to find out who did the murder or other criminal act. In *Dr Jekyll and Mr Hyde*, we know who murdered Sir Danvers Carew. The mystery is that nobody can find Mr Hyde, the murderer; he has completely disappeared.

Because the Jekyll and Hyde story has been used so much in films and plays, we know the general idea: that Dr Jekyll discovers a chemical mixture that will separate the evil part of himself into a different body – "Mr Hyde". There is – for us – no real mystery about that. But see how, in Stevenson's book, the first readers discovered it. It is only in the last two chapters, in Henry Jekyll's confession, that the reader learns the truth. He or she may have guessed the answer. There are plenty of clues – things that help the reader to guess it. But (for the first readers) the secret is kept until the end.

Chapter 1
The door

Mr John Utterson was a lawyer in London. He seemed to be a cold man, without feeling. He never smiled, and he spoke only when it was necessary. But people liked him. There was something in his eyes that showed his understanding of other people. He understood, and he never blamed them. Men and women came to him for his advice or help in matters of law, and he treated them all equally.

Mr Utterson's friends seemed to be equal in his eyes too. They were people of his own family and people he had known for a long time. He did not expect them to earn their places in his circle of friends.

Other people could not see a reason for Mr Utterson and Mr Richard Enfield to be friends.

"What do they see in each other?" people asked. "What do they talk about when they are together?"

And the answer was: "If you see them on their Sunday walks, they are never saying anything. They don't seem to be enjoying themselves at all."

But the fact is, the two men thought their Sunday walks were an important part of the week. They enjoyed the walks, and they enjoyed each other's company, although often it was silent company.

It happened that on one of their walks they went down a narrow street. It was a quiet street on a Sunday, but during the week the little shops on each side were very busy. Because the shops were successful, they were clean and brightly painted, and the street itself was clean. It was a pleasant street to walk along.

Mr Enfield points to the door with his walking-stick

Near one end of this street, there was a break in the line of shops. There was a narrow entrance to a court-yard, and beside it the windowless end of an ugly build-ing. A door in this wall was unpainted and in need of repair.

Mr Enfield and the lawyer were on the other side of the street, but Mr Enfield pointed to it with his walking-stick.

"Have you ever noticed that door, John?" he asked.

"Yes. Ugly, isn't it?"

"Every time I pass it," said Mr Enfield, "I remember something very curious that happened."

"Oh?" said Mr Utterson. "What happened?"

Chapter 2
Mr Enfield's story

One dark winter morning, I was on my way home at about three o'clock. I had walked a very long way without seeing anyone at all. Everybody was asleep. Suddenly I saw not one but two figures. One was a little man who was walking quickly towards the cross-road there. The other was a little girl, about eight years old, who was running as quickly as she could out of the cross-road. The two met at the corner. And then I saw something quite terrible. The girl fell down, and the man calmly walked on her, stepping on her body, paying no attention to her cries. It wasn't like a man – more like a mindless machine. He walked on. I gave a shout, ran after him, caught him by the neck, and brought him back.

A group of people had gathered round the crying child. The man was quite calm, and he didn't try to escape. But he gave me one look, and it made my blood run cold. I felt myself hating him.

The people who had gathered were the girl's own family, and soon they were joined by the doctor who had been sent for. The girl was not greatly harmed – more frightened, the doctor said. But there was something very unusual in the situation. I had felt an immediate hate for the man I was holding. The child's family hated him too, and that was natural. But the doctor was not like us. He was the usual self-controlled medical man with more sense than imagination. And yet, every time he looked at the man, I saw him turn sick and white with the wish to kill him.

I saw what was in the doctor's mind, just as he knew

what was in mine. We couldn't kill the man, even if we wanted to, but we promised to make as much trouble for him as we could. We said we would make his action known everywhere. And all the time, we were keeping the women away from him. They were so angry that they were wild and dangerous. I never saw a circle of such hate-filled faces. And there was the man, in the middle, cool and scornful – but frightened, too.

"If you want money," he said, "say how much. No gentleman wants trouble with people like you."

We told him we would take a hundred pounds for the child and her family. He didn't want to agree, but the little crowd round him looked so dangerous that he said he would pay. The next thing was to get the money, and where do you think he led us to? To that place with the door! He pulled a key out of his pocket, and went in. After a time, he came out with ten pounds in coins, and a cheque for the rest. The cheque was signed, and the signature surprised me. It was the name of a famous man! I can't tell you the name, but it was very well known and honoured.

"I don't like this," I said. "It's most unusual for a man to walk through a door like that at four o'clock in the morning, and come out of it with another man's cheque for nearly a hundred pounds."

But he answered scornfully, "You needn't worry. I'll stay with you till the banks open, and I'll get the money for the cheque myself." He did that, and the bank paid the money without question.

Chapter 3
The cheque

Mr Utterson looked surprised at this story.

"I see you feel the same as I do," said Mr Enfield. "It's a surprising story. The man who hurt the girl was a very nasty fellow, the sort of man that good people don't deal with. And the man who signed the cheque is just the opposite, a really good man, and very well known too."

"What is the name of the man who walked over the child?" asked Mr Utterson.

"His name," Mr Enfield said, "is Mr Hyde."

"And you don't know if the man who signed the cheque lives there?"

"Behind that door?" Mr Enfield said. "No. His house is in a square, though I don't remember its name. The place behind the door doesn't really seem like a house. There are three windows on the first floor over the courtyard. They are always shut, but they're clean. And there is a chimney that's usually smoking. So somebody must live there. But the houses are all so close together round the courtyard that you can't be sure where one ends and another begins. There doesn't seem to be another door, and nobody uses the door I showed you, except the man I have told you about."

Mr Utterson walked on in silence. It was clear that he was thinking. At last he said, "You are sure he used a key?" Mr Enfield was clearly surprised, and the lawyer went on: "I'm sorry. It must seem a strange question, but there is a reason for it. You see, I already know the name of the man who signed the cheque."

Chapter 4
Who is Mr Hyde?

That evening, Mr Utterson ate his dinner without much
interest. Then he took a candle and went into his
business room. There he opened his safe and took out
an envelope marked "Dr Jekyll's Will". He sat down and
began to read the will with a look on his face of great
displeasure.

The will was in Dr Jekyll's own writing because Mr
Utterson had refused to help him with it. It was the
lawyer's duty to keep it for the doctor, but it had been
made without his advice – indeed against his advice. The
will said clearly that if Henry Jekyll died, everything
he owned had to pass into the hands of his "friend and
helper Edward Hyde", and if Dr Jekyll "disappeared or,
without explanation, was not seen for three months", the
same Edward Hyde should take Henry Jekyll's place
immediately.

The lawyer had always disliked this will. It displeased
him as a lawyer, and it made him angry as a person who
liked people to behave in an ordinary way. His dislike
had been strong enough when Hyde was only a name.
Now he had heard some very unpleasant things about the
man with that name.

"I thought it was madness," he told himself. "Now it
seems like something much worse."

He put the will back in his safe, put on a coat, and
went out to visit his friend, the famous Dr Lanyon. "If
anyone knows," he thought, "it will be Lanyon."

Dr Lanyon's butler was glad to see Mr Utterson, and
led him straight to the dining-room, where Dr Lanyon

was just finishing his dinner. As soon as he saw Mr Utterson, the doctor jumped up and took his friend's hands. They had known and liked each other for a long time, at school and at university, and they enjoyed each other's company. The doctor was a big, cheerful man, healthy and red-faced.

After a little general talk, the lawyer spoke about Dr Jekyll.

"I suppose, Lanyon," he said, "you and I must be the two oldest friends that Henry Jekyll has."

"I wish the friends were younger," said Dr Lanyon, smiling. "But yes, I suppose we are, though I don't see him often now."

"Oh? I thought you were both interested in the same scientific work."

"We were," Dr Lanyon replied, "but Henry Jekyll began to let his imagination spoil his science."

"Oh!" thought Utterson. "They have quarrelled – but only on a matter of science." He waited for a moment, then asked the question he had come to ask. "Did you ever meet a man he knows – by the name of Hyde?"

"Hyde?" said Lanyon, and immediately: "No. I never heard Henry Jekyll say that name."

Mr Utterson went home, but Enfield's story would not leave his mind. "I must see this Mr Hyde," he thought. "I must see this man who has the power to make Enfield hate him so strongly – this man who seems to have such power over Henry Jekyll."

From that time, Mr Utterson began to watch the door in the street of little shops whenever he had time. And at last, at about ten o'clock one night, he heard some quick steps coming towards the door.

Mr Utterson stepped into the entrance to the court-yard. From there, he could see that the man who was coming was small, and dressed in very plain clothes. He could not see the man's face at all clearly, but he still felt a strong dislike for him.

The man walked straight towards the door, taking a key from his pocket.

Mr Utterson moved out and touched him on the shoulder. "Mr Hyde, I think?"

Mr Hyde moved a step away, taking in a quick breath. But if he was afraid, his fear did not last more than a moment. Although he did not look at the lawyer's face, he said quite coolly: "That is my name. What do you want?"

"I see that you are going in," the lawyer answered. "I am an old friend of Dr Jekyll's. I am sure you have heard my name: Utterson. I thought that you might be willing to save me a longer walk by letting me go in through this door."

"You won't find Dr Jekyll at home," replied Mr Hyde. "He is out." And then suddenly, but still without looking up, he said, "How did you know me?"

"Before I answer that question, will you let me see your face?"

Mr Hyde seemed to think for a moment. Then he turned round and stared straight at Mr Utterson.

"Thank you," said Utterson. "Now I'll know you again."

"Yes. And you can have my address, too." And he gave Utterson a card with an address in Soho.

Mr Utterson was surprised. "Why," he wondered, "has he given me his address? Is he thinking of Henry Jekyll's will?" But he did not show his feelings, just

Mr Hyde stares straight at Mr Utterson

putting the card in his pocket and saying something that could have been, "Thanks."

"And now," Hyde said. "I'll repeat my question. How did you know me?"

"By description."

"Who described me?"

Mr Utterson thought quickly. "There are people who know both of us."

"Who are they?"

"Jekyll is one," said the lawyer.

"He never told you about me," cried Mr Hyde angrily. "I didn't expect you to tell me a lie!" he said. And moving surprisingly quickly, he went to the door, unlocked it, and disappeared into the house.

Mr Utterson walked slowly away, turning a problem over in his mind. Mr Hyde was pale and small. He had a displeasing smile. He had spoken to the lawyer in a whispering, rather broken voice, mixing politeness, scorn and rough manners. But these were not important matters. They did not explain the feelings of fear and hate that filled Mr Utterson when the man was near him.

"It's something in the soul of the man – some terrible evil," the lawyer thought. "Poor Henry Jekyll! Your new friend is the nearest thing to a devil that I have ever met."

Round the corner at the end of the street of small shops there was a square of old houses. They had nearly all become flats and offices, but one house, the second from the corner, was still owned by one person. It looked well cared for and comfortable. Mr Utterson went to the door of this house and knocked. A well-dressed, rather old butler opened the door.

"Is Dr Jekyll at home, Poole?" asked the lawyer.

"I'll go and see, Mr Utterson," said Poole. And he showed the lawyer into the hall and pointed to a big chair. "Would you like to sit there, sir? I won't be long."

Mr Utterson thought about what he was going to say to his friend. He was really rather glad when Poole came back after a time and said that Dr Jekyll had gone out.

"I saw Mr Hyde go in by the old workroom door, Poole," he said. "Is it right for him to do that, when Dr Jekyll is out?"

"Yes, it's quite right, sir," said the butler. "Mr Hyde has a key."

"Hm! Your master seems to trust that young man, Poole."

"Yes, sir. He does," said Poole. "We all have orders to obey Mr Hyde."

"I don't think I have ever met Mr Hyde here."

"Oh, no, sir. He never comes to *dinner* here," replied the butler. "Indeed we very seldom see him on this side of the house. He usually comes and goes by the workroom."

"Well, good night, Poole."

"Good night, Mr Utterson."

The lawyer started to walk home very sadly. "Poor Henry Jekyll," he thought. "I'm afraid he's in trouble of some sort. He was rather wild when he was a young man. Can it be that some old wrongdoing has come from the past to destroy him?"

Hyde's freedom to come and go in Jekyll's house worried Utterson. "If that evil fellow learns about the will," he thought, "he may want to hurry Jekyll's death or disappearance. Then he would enjoy the things that Jekyll owns at present. I must do something about it – if Jekyll will let me – *if* he will let me."

Chapter 5
After dinner

Mr Utterson was very glad when, about two weeks later, Dr Jekyll gave one of his pleasant dinners to five or six old friends. As usual, the lawyer stayed after the others had gone. His friends liked to sit in his quiet company, his rich silence.

As they sat together on each side of the fire, you could see that Dr Jekyll was truly fond of his old friend.

"I have been wanting to speak to you, Jekyll," Utterson began. "It's about that will of yours."

It was clear that the doctor did not like the subject. But he smiled. "My poor Utterson," he said. "I'm very sorry to cause you so much worry."

"You know I never liked that will."

"Yes. I know that," said the doctor, rather sharply. "You have told me so."

"Well, I tell you so again. I have been learning something about young Hyde."

Dr Jekyll's face grew pale. "I don't want to hear any more," he said.

"What I heard was very bad."

"It can't make any difference," said the doctor. "You don't understand the situation. It's a very strange situation, Utterson – very strange. And talking about it won't make it any better."

"Henry," said Utterson, "you know me, and you know you can trust me. Tell me all about it, and I am sure I can get you out of the trouble, whatever it is."

"It's good of you. You're a really good man, Utterson, and I can't find words to thank you. I would trust you more than any other person. But it isn't what you think. I can tell you one thing: whenever I want to – the moment I choose – I can get rid of Hyde. But because we have talked about the subject – for the last time, I hope – there is one thing I want you to know. I am truly interested in poor Hyde. I know you have seen him; he told me so. And I am afraid he was not polite. But I do take a great interest in that young man. I want to ask you to help him to get the things that are in my will. Can you give me that promise?"

"I can't pretend that I will ever like him," said the lawyer.

"I don't ask for that," said Jekyll, putting his hand on his old friend's arm. "I only ask for fair treatment. I only want you, as my friend, to help him when I have gone."

Utterson looked very unhappy. But at last he said, "All right. I promise."

Chapter 6
The Carew murder

Nearly a year later, in October 1880, there was a fearful crime in a London street.

A young woman servant saw it happen. She had gone up to her room at about eleven o'clock that night, and she was standing at the window, looking out at the moonlit streets. She noticed an old gentleman with white hair coming along the narrow street below her window.

There was another – a very small – man going along the street in the opposite direction. She hardly noticed him at first. When the two men were quite near to each other, the old man bowed and seemed to ask a polite question. The girl saw him pointing, and she thought he was asking the way, but the moon was shining on his face, and she was watching that. It seemed such a kind, peaceful face.

She looked at the other man. To her surprise, she knew him. He was a man called Mr Hyde, who had once visited her master. She remembered that she had felt a strong dislike for him. He had a heavy stick in his hand.

Suddenly this Mr Hyde became madly angry, waving his stick and shouting. The old gentleman looked most surprised. He took a step back. And then Mr Hyde really went mad (as the girl described it), striking the old man over the head with his stick, and beating him to the ground. The next moment he jumped on the old man's body and struck him again and again with the heavy stick. The girl heard the bones breaking and saw the old man's body thrown about by the sharp movements of death.

These terrible sights and sounds were too much for the girl. She lost consciousness.

It was two o'clock when the girl became conscious again and called for the police. The murderer had gone, but the murdered man still lay in the middle of the narrow street, a terribly broken and wounded body. The stick that the murderer had used had broken in the middle although it was of an unusually hard, strong wood. One half of it lay near the body. The police found some money and a gold watch in the murdered man's pockets, and there was a letter that he had probably been taking to the post. The envelope had Mr Utterson's name and address on it.

A police officer brought this letter to the lawyer in the morning.

"This is very serious," Mr Utterson said, "but I don't want to say any more until I have seen the body."

The body had been taken to the police station. As soon as Utterson saw it, he said, "Yes. I know him. I am afraid there is no doubt. It is Sir Danvers Carew."

"Really, sir?" said the police officer. "A very famous man." And his eyes showed the sudden hope that he might himself become famous if he caught the murderer. "Perhaps," he said, "you will be able to help us to find the man, sir." And he told Utterson what the girl had seen, and showed him the broken stick.

Mr Utterson had already been shaken when he heard the name of Hyde. When he saw the stick, he knew there could be no doubt. The stick was badly broken, but he knew it. He himself had given it to Henry Jekyll many years before.

"Is this Mr Hyde a small man?" he asked.

The girl sees Mr Hyde beat the old man

"Yes," said the officer, "very small, and very evil-looking, the servant-girl says."

Mr Utterson thought for a moment. Then: "If you will come with me in my carriage," he said, "I think I can take you to his house."

The address that Hyde had given was in an unpleasant part of Soho. The door was opened by an old woman.

"Yes," she said, "this is Mr Hyde's house, but Mr Hyde is not at home." And in answer to questions from Mr Utterson she said that Hyde had been in very late the night before. That wasn't unusual. He came and went at all sorts of times, and he was often away. For example, until last night she had not seen him for more than two months.

"Well," said Mr Utterson, "we want to see his rooms."

"That's impossible——" the woman began.

Mr Utterson stopped her. "This person," he said, "is Police Inspector Newcome from Scotland Yard."

A nasty look of joy appeared on the woman's face. "Ah!" she said. "Mr Hyde is in trouble! What has he done?"

The inspector did not answer. "Just let us look," he said.

The rooms had good furniture, curtains and carpets. But it was clear that they had been very hurriedly cleared of certain things. There were clothes lying on the floor with the pockets turned out. Drawers were open. And in the fireplace a lot of papers had been burnt. The burning had been hurried, and there were unburnt remains. From them the inspector pulled out a part of a cheque book.

"Now we've got him," the police officer said. "All we

have to do is wait for him at the bank. He can't do anything without money."

It was not so easy. Mr Hyde did not go near the bank. Nor was it possible to get a good description of the man. He had never been photographed. And the people who could describe him gave widely different descriptions. They all agreed on only one point: there was something that made them hate him.

Chapter 7
The letter

It was late in the afternoon when Mr Utterson went to Dr Jekyll's house. Poole opened the door to him, and soon the lawyer and the butler were crossing a yard behind the house. It had once been the garden, but now its only purpose was to lead to the building that was called the workroom.

The workroom itself was arranged for experiments with chemicals. Above it there was a large room in which the doctor had his desk, hundreds of books, and more things for experiments. There was a fire in the fireplace. Near it, Dr Jekyll was sitting, looking very ill.

As soon as Poole had left them, Mr Utterson said, "You have heard the news?"

"Yes," said the doctor through white lips. "The newspaper boys were shouting it out in the streets."

"Then tell me one thing," said the lawyer. "Carew was my client, but so are you, and I want to know what I am doing. You haven't been so mad as to hide this fellow?"

"Utterson, I swear that I will never see him again. It is all at an end. I'll never have any more dealings with him. He is quite safe, and nobody will ever hear of him again."

The lawyer was very worried by his friend's appearance and way of speaking. Dr Jekyll seemed very ill. "You seem sure, Henry," Utterson said. "I hope you are right. If they caught the man and tried him, your name would come into the trial."

"I am quite sure," Jekyll answered. "I have good

Dr Jekyll in the room above his workroom

21

reasons to be sure, though I can't give anybody those reasons. But there is one thing you can advise me about. I ... I have had a letter, and I don't know whether to show it to the police. I want to put it in your hands, Utterson. I know your advice will be good."

"You are afraid it may help the police to catch him?"

"No," said the doctor. "I don't care what happens to Hyde. I have finished with him – completely finished. I was thinking of my own name."

"Well, " said the lawyer, "let me see the letter."

The letter was written in an unusual, unsloping hand-writing:

Dear Dr Jekyll,

You have helped me in so many ways, and I am afraid I have paid you for your kindness by behaving very badly. But you may want to know that you need have no fear about my being safe. I have a way of escape that is entirely sure.

Please forgive and forget me.

Edward Hyde

Mr Utterson liked the letter. It showed that his worst fears about the situation were mistaken.

"Do you have the envelope?" he asked.

"I burnt it without thinking," Jekyll answered. "But there was no postmark on it. Somebody brought it to the house."

Mr Utterson thought for a moment. Then he said, "If you agree, I'll keep the letter until tomorrow and think about it. And now, one more question: it was Hyde who wanted you to put that sentence in your will about your disappearing, was it?"

The doctor's "Yes" could hardly be heard.

"I knew it," said Utterson. "He was going to murder you. You have had a lucky escape."

"I've had something much more important," the doctor said solemnly. "I've had a lesson. Oh, Utterson, what a lesson I have had!"

On his way out, the lawyer stopped in the hall and spoke to Poole. "Somebody brought a letter for the doctor this morning, Poole," he said. "Can you describe the person who brought it?"

"No letters have come today," the old butler said, "except a few that the postman brought – all bills."

Mr Utterson's fears were as great as before, as he walked home. The letter, it seemed, had come by the workroom door. "Perhaps it was written in the workroom building," he thought. "If that is so, I must be very careful."

The newspaper boys were shouting, "Special! Terrible murder of a Member of Parliament!"

A few hours later, Mr Utterson was sitting by the fire in his own business room. With him was his head clerk, Mr Guest. He kept very few secrets from Guest. Guest had often been to Dr Jekyll's house on business. He knew Poole. Perhaps he knew about Mr Hyde's visits to the house. Utterson thought it might be wise to show him the letter which explained some of the mystery. But the reason the lawyer gave for showing Guest the letter was that Guest was very clever about handwriting.

"This is terrible news about Sir Danvers Carew," Mr Utterson said.

"Yes, sir, terrible. The murderer was mad, of course."

"I'd like to hear what you think about that," the lawyer said. "I have a letter here in his handwriting. Will you look at it? It's just what you might be interested in: a murderer's handwriting. I'm not quite sure what to do about the letter, and at the moment it must be a secret between the two of us. But I'd like to hear your opinion about the handwriting."

Guest's eyes brightened, and he studied the letter with great interest. "No, sir," he said. "Not mad. But it's very curious handwriting."

Just then, the servant came in with a note for Mr Utterson.

"Is that from Dr Jekyll, sir?" the clerk asked. "I thought I knew the writing. Is it private, Mr Utterson?"

"Only asking me to come to dinner. Why? Do you want to see it?"

"Just for a moment, sir, if you please." And the clerk put the two pieces of paper side by side and studied them with great interest.

"Thank you, sir," he said at last, and he gave both the notes back to Mr·Utterson.

There was a moment of silence. Then the lawyer asked the question that Guest was expecting. Mr Utterson was afraid that he already knew the answer. "Why did you look at the two together, Guest?"

"Well, sir, in very many ways the handwriting is the same. The only real difference is in the slope."

"Rather curious," said Utterson.

"Yes. As you say, rather curious."

"It isn't something to mention to other people."

"No, sir," said the clerk. "I understand."

As soon as Mr Utterson was alone, he locked the note in his safe. "I don't understand it," he thought. "Henry Jekyll writing a false letter for a murderer!" And the blood ran cold through his body.

Guest studies the letter with great interest

Chapter 8
Dr Lanyon

Time ran on. Thousands of pounds were offered for information about Sir Danvers Carew's murderer. But Mr Hyde had disappeared completely. The police heard a great deal about his past. They heard stories about his cruelty, his crimes, his nasty friends, the hate that people felt when they met him. There was no news at all about where he had gone. From the time he had left the house in Soho on the morning of the murder, Mr Hyde was not heard of.

Mr Utterson slowly became less worried as the time passed. And he saw that a new life had begun for his friend Dr Jekyll with the disappearance of Mr Hyde. The doctor gathered his old friends around him, and there were dinners and cheerful talk as in the old days.

On the eighth of January, Utterson had dinner at Jekyll's house with a small party. Dr Lanyon was there, and Henry Jekyll looked from him to Utterson as in the days when the three friends could hardly be separated.

On the twelfth of January, and again on the fourteenth, Utterson tried to see his friend.

"The doctor is unable to leave the house, sir," said Poole. "He can't receive visitors."

On the fifteenth of January, Utterson tried again, with the same result. He was worried. For two months he had seen his friend almost every day, and he was unhappy at the change.

At last he went to see Dr Lanyon. He thought the doctor's butler looked anxious, but the man led him immediately to his master.

Mr Utterson was shocked at the change in his friend. The usually healthy-looking man was pale. He looked much older and thinner. The lawyer was sure he was dying. But it was not the signs of bodily illness that shocked him so much as the look in the doctor's eyes – a look of terrible fear, of something in the mind that was killing him.

"You don't look well," said the lawyer. "Is it something serious, old friend?"

"I have had a shock," said Dr Lanyon. And then he added, with no uncertainty in his voice, "I won't get better. I expect to die in a few weeks. Well – life has been pleasant. I have enjoyed it. – Yes, I used to like it. I sometimes think that if we knew everything, we would be more glad to leave this life."

"Jekyll is ill, too," said Utterson. "Have you seen him?"

Lanyon held up a hand that was shaking with weakness or strong feelings. "I don't want to see Dr Jekyll again or to hear anything about him," he said.

"That's very sad," Utterson said. "Isn't there anything I can do to help? We have been three very good friends, Lanyon, and we are too old to make other friends."

"No," said Lanyon. "You can't do anything. Ask him."

"He won't see me," said the lawyer.

"I'm not surprised," was the reply. "Some day soon, Utterson, after I am dead, you may perhaps learn the truth about this. I can't tell you. Just now, if you can sit and talk with me about other things, that will be good. If you can't avoid that subject, please go, because I can't bear it."

As soon as he got home, Utterson sat down and wrote a letter to Jekyll. He said that he was unhappy not to be allowed to see the doctor, and he asked the doctor about the cause of the quarrel with Lanyon.

A long answer came the next day. It was very sad, and in places very mysterious. Towards the end, Utterson read:

> There is nothing that will end the quarrel between Lanyon and me. I do not blame an old friend, but I agree with him that we must never meet again. From now on, I am going to see very few people. You must not doubt that I am still your friend if my door is shut even to you. You must allow me to go my own dark way. I have earned for myself a punishment and danger that I cannot name. My suffering and terrors are worse than I can describe, and you can lighten them for me, Utterson, only by understanding my silence.

Utterson could not understand the sudden change. It looked like madness, but the lawyer remembered Lanyon's words, and he knew that there must be some less simple cause.

A week later, Dr Lanyon was in bed, and two weeks after that, he was dead. Mr Utterson was very sad about the loss of his old friend as he sat down in his business room to deal with an envelope marked:

PRIVATE. For the eyes of J G Utterson ONLY.

That was in Dr Lanyon's writing. Inside the envelope there was another. It was marked, again in Dr Lanyon's writing:

NOT to be opened until the death or disappearance of Dr Henry Jekyll.

Mr Utterson could hardly believe his eyes. Here was the idea of "disappearance" again, as in the will that he had given back to Dr Jekyll several weeks ago. It had been put into the will at the suggestion of the evil man Hyde, but here it was in Dr Lanyon's handwriting. Utterson wanted to open the envelope and read, but his honour as a lawyer did not allow him to do that: he locked it in the back of his safe, unopened.

He went quite often to Dr Jekyll's house, but he did not see the doctor. Poole, at the door, had no good news to give him. The doctor spent nearly all his time in the room above the workroom, Poole said. Sometimes he even slept there. He had grown very silent, and his servants were all very worried about him.

Chapter 9
At the window

One Sunday, on their usual walk, Mr Utterson and Mr Enfield found themselves entering the narrow street where Dr Jekyll's workroom door was.

They stopped and looked at the door.

"Well," said Enfield, "that story's at an end. We won't see Mr Hyde again."

"I hope not," said Utterson. "Did I ever tell you that I once saw him? And I had the same feelings of fear and hate as you described."

"Everybody seemed to have the same feelings," Enfield replied. "When I told you about what happened here, I didn't know that this was a back way to Dr Jekyll's house."

"Well, let's step into the courtyard and look at the windows. I must tell you that I am anxious about poor Jekyll. Even if we can't go in, it might be good for him to hear a friend's voice."

The middle one of the three windows was half-open. Utterson saw Jekyll sitting close to it. He looked very sad, like an unhappy prisoner.

"Hello!" called Utterson. "Jekyll! I hope you're better."

"I'm unwell, Utterson," the doctor answered weakly, "very unwell. Thank God it won't last long."

"You stay inside too much," the lawyer said. "You should be out, getting your blood moving, like Enfield and me. Come on. Get your hat and come for a quick walk with us."

The doctor came closer to the window. "You are very

good," he said. "I should like to very much. But no, it's quite impossible. I daren't. But indeed, Utterson, I'm very glad to see you. It's a real pleasure. I would ask you and Mr Enfield to come up, but the place is really not fit."

"Well, then," Utterson said, "the best thing we can do is to stay down here and talk to you from where we are."

Dr Jekyll smiled. "I was just going to suggest that," he said. But the words were hardly out when the smile seemed to be struck from his face. In its place came a look of such hopeless terror that the two men below felt their blood freeze. They saw it only for a moment, because the window was immediately shut. But that moment had been enough. They both turned and left the courtyard without saying a word. It was not until they reached a street that was quite busy, even on a Sunday, that Mr Utterson at last turned and looked at his friend. They were both pale, and there was a shocked look in their eyes.

"God forgive us!" said Mr Utterson.

Mr Enfield only moved his head in solemn agreement, and the two walked on again in silence.

Chapter 10
The last night

Mr Utterson was sitting alone one evening after dinner. He was surprised when Poole came to see him.

"Hullo, Poole," he said, "what's this visit about?" And then when he had looked again at Dr Jekyll's butler: "What's the matter? Is the doctor ill?"

"Mr Utterson," Poole said, "something is terribly wrong."

"Sit down and tell me about it," said the lawyer. "Where is the doctor?"

"Well, sir, that's the trouble. You know he shuts himself up in the room above the workroom. But something's wrong – terribly wrong. I'm afraid, Mr Utterson. I've been afraid for a week, and I can't bear it any more."

Utterson said, "What do you mean? What are you afraid of, Poole?"

"I daren't say, sir," said Poole. "But will you come with me – please, sir – please – and see for yourself?"

Mr Utterson's only answer was to get his hat and coat. He was surprised to see the result of this action in the butler's face – as if a great load had been taken off his shoulders.

When they reached Dr Jekyll's front door, Poole knocked in a special way, and a voice from inside asked, "Is that you, Mr Poole?"

"It's all right," said Poole. "Mr Utterson's here. Open the door."

All Dr Jekyll's servants were in the hall.

"Why are you all here?" Utterson wanted to know.

"They're all afraid," said Poole. No one disagreed with that. "Will you come with me, sir?" the butler went on. "We'll need this candle. Will you come as quietly as you can, Mr Utterson? I want you to hear, and I don't want you to be heard." And he led the way to the yard at the back of the house. "One more thing, sir," Poole said. "If he asks you to go in, don't go, sir, please."

They went through the workroom to the foot of the stairs. Here Poole whispered to Mr Utterson to stand on one side and listen. He himself went up the stairs and knocked on the door with an uncertain hand.

"Mr Utterson, sir, is asking to see you," Poole called, and at the same time he showed by signs that the lawyer should listen.

A voice came from the other side of the door: "Tell him I can't see anyone."

"Thank you, sir," said Poole, and he led Mr Utterson back to the house.

"Sir," he said, looking into the lawyer's eyes, "was that my master's voice?"

"It seems greatly changed," Utterson replied.

"Changed?" said the butler. "I have been twenty years in Dr Jekyll's house, and I know his voice. That isn't it. No, sir. My master has been killed. He was killed a week ago, when we heard him cry to God. Who is there instead of him, Mr Utterson? And why does he stay there?"

"But if Dr Jekyll has been murdered, as you suppose, what would make the murderer stay? It doesn't make sense."

"No, it doesn't make sense," Poole agreed. "But there's more to tell you. All this week, the person or thing that lives in that room has been crying day and night for some sort of medicine, and he can't get what he wants. Dr Jekyll used sometimes to write his orders on a piece of paper and throw it on the stairs. We've had nothing else for a week but orders of that kind – nothing but papers and a closed door. There have been orders for meals, which were taken in when nobody was looking. But mostly there were orders for a chemical. I have taken these orders to every chemicals merchant in London. And every time I brought the stuff back, there was another paper telling me to take it back because it wasn't pure. I don't know what the chemical is for, sir, but it is wanted very badly."

"Do you have any of those papers, Poole?"

"Yes, sir. The man at Maw and Company was very angry and threw this one back at me."

Mr Utterson read the note:

Maw and Company:

The last supply of the chemical I have asked you for was impure and quite useless to me. In the year 1875 I bought quite a large amount of this chemical from you. Now I must ask you to make a very careful search. If there is any of the same chemical without impurities in your stores, please send it to me at once. The cost does not matter. This is very important.

This part of the note did not show any great excitement, but the last sentence showed very strong feelings. The pen had nearly torn the paper as the writer ended:

For God's sake, find me some of the old.

"It certainly seems to be Dr Jekyll's writing," said Mr Utterson.

"Yes," said Poole, "but it *isn't* Dr Jekyll up there. I've seen him!"

"Seen him?"

"Yes, sir. I came suddenly into the workroom from the garden, and there he was. I suppose he had come down secretly into the workroom to look for this chemical. His face was covered, and he was searching madly among the boxes in the workroom. When he saw me, he gave a cry and ran up the stairs to the room above. My master wouldn't do that. This person's face was covered, but it wasn't my master. Dr Jekyll is a tall, strongly-built man; the man I saw was small, and when I saw him I felt sick."

Mr Utterson looked at the butler, who had clearly been terribly frightened. "We must speak openly to each other, Poole," he said. "This person with the covered face: did you know who it was?"

"You mean, was it Mr Hyde? Yes, sir, I think it was. The person was his size, with his quick movements. And he gave you the feeling that he was all evil."

"Poole," said the lawyer, "I see that it is my duty to break down the door of the room above the workroom."

"Oh, sir," Poole cried, "I'm very glad to hear you say that. I'll come with you. There's an axe and an iron bar in the workroom."

They sent two menservants to watch the door that opened into the narrow street. Then Mr Utterson and Poole went to the door of the room.

"Jekyll," cried Utterson loudly, "I must see you."

There was no answer.

"If you don't open the door," called the lawyer, "we'll break it down."

"Utterson," they heard from the other side of the door, "for God's sake have pity!"

"That's not Jekyll's voice," said Utterson. "It's Hyde's. The door must come down."

It was a very well made door, very strong, and they had to use the axe several times before at last the lock broke and the door was open.

The room, in the quiet candlelight, was in good order. Except for the cupboards full of chemicals and the tables for scientific work, it looked like any other room. But on the floor, right in the middle of the room, was the body of a man. It was cruelly bent, and there were still sharp movements of the arms and legs. The two men moved to it with some fear, and turned it on its back.

The face was Edward Hyde's. He was dressed in clothes that were many sizes too big for him – clothes for a man of Dr Jekyll's size. Parts of his face were still making sharp movements, but he was quite dead. The broken glass in his hand and the strong smell made it clear that he had taken his own life, by poison.

"We have come too late," Utterson said – "too late for Hyde to be punished, and too late to save your master. All we can do is find the body of Dr Jekyll."

They searched the building, but nowhere could they find the body. The door into the narrow street was locked, and the key lay broken on the floor just inside the door.

They went back to the room where the body of Mr Hyde lay. On the desk, there was a large envelope. It had the name "Mr Utterson" written on it in Dr Jekyll's handwriting. The lawyer opened it. Three things fell out.

Mr Utterson and Poole find Mr Hyde dead

The first was a will. Like Dr Jekyll's first will, it mentioned his death or disappearance, but the name of the person to receive everything was not Edward Hyde. The lawyer was most surprised to read in its place the name "John Utterson".

Utterson looked at Poole, then back at the papers, then at the body on the floor.

"I don't understand at all," he said. "Hyde has been here all this time. He had no reason to like me. He would have been very angry to see my name taking the place of his. But he hasn't destroyed this."

He picked up the next paper. It was a short note in the doctor's handwriting, and the date was at the top.

"Poole!" he cried, "Dr Jekyll was here and alive today! He's still alive, because no one could get rid of a body so quickly. He must have escaped! But why? And how? There are a lot of difficulties here. If we tell people about this death, we may make a great deal of trouble for your master. Oh, we must be careful!"

"Why don't you read the note, sir?" asked Poole.

"Because I'm afraid," replied the lawyer solemnly. "I hope I have no reason to be afraid, but ——" He looked at the note:

My dear Utterson,

When this is in your hands, I will have disappeared. I don't know how it will happen – only that it will happen, soon and quite certainly. So please go, and first read the paper that Lanyon warned me he was going to give you. And then, if you want to know more, read my confession.

Your unhappy friend,

Henry Jekyll

"Where's the third thing?" asked Utterson.

"Here, sir." Poole picked up from the floor a thick envelope and passed it to the lawyer.

Utterson put it in his pocket. "Let's say nothing about this yet. If your master has escaped or is dead, we may at least save his good name. It's ten o'clock now. I must go home and read these papers in a quiet place. But I'll be back before midnight, and then we'll send for the police."

They went out, locking the door of the workroom behind them. And Utterson walked home to read the two papers which were to explain the mystery.

Chapter 11
Dr Lanyon's story

On the ninth of January, four days ago, I, Dr Hastie Lanyon, received in the evening post a registered letter. My name and address on the envelope were in the handwriting of my fellow-doctor and old school friend, Henry Jekyll.

I was surprised by this because we hardly ever wrote letters to each other. I had seen the man, and had dinner with him, the night before, and we had not talked about anything so important as to make him register a letter to me. This was the letter:

9 December 1881

Dear Lanyon,

You are one of my oldest friends. I have always been fond of you. If you had ever said to me, "Jekyll, my life, my honour, my mind are in danger," I would have done anything to help you.

Now, Lanyon, *my* life, *my* honour and *my* mind are all in great danger. If you don't help me tonight, I am lost.

This is what I ask you to do. As soon as you have read this letter, drive straight to my house. Poole, my butler, has orders to be waiting for you. He will take you to the door of my room above the work-room. I want you to go in alone. Open the cupboard marked "E" on the left (break the lock if necessary). Pull out the fourth drawer from the top. It contains some powders, a bottle, and a note-book. Please carry this drawer, *with everything in it*, to your house.

At midnight, I ask you to be alone in your work-room. A man will come, mentioning my name. Please give him the drawer. That is all I ask you to do. Five minutes afterwards, you will have understood how important this is to me. I don't believe you will fail me; the result would be my death or madness. But I am sure you will do what I ask, and earn all my thanks.

Yours, H.J.

When I read that letter, I was sure the doctor was mad. But until that was proved, I knew I must do what he asked. I drove immediately to Jekyll's house. The butler was waiting for me; he, too, had received a registered letter with his orders from Dr Jekyll.

The cupboard marked "E" was not locked. I took out the drawer, covered it with a cloth, and brought it back to my house.

I looked at the things in the drawer. They were as Jekyll had described them. The powders looked like a mixture that he had measured and put in separate papers. The notebook contained very little except dates. There was sometimes a short note after the date: "double" is an example, and once, early in the list, "completely failed!!!" It did not seem to me that my bringing these things to my house could do anything for the life, the honour or the mind of the doctor. It looked more and more like madness.

I sent the servants to bed, and at midnight I was waiting alone in my workroom with the drawer – and a gun out of sight.

There was a quiet knock at the door. I opened it, and

found a small man trying to keep in the dark near the door.

"Are you from Dr Jekyll?" I asked.

He made a sign that I understood as "Yes", and I told him to come in. He was watching a policeman coming into the square on the far side, and hurried inside, clearly in fear.

In the bright light of my workroom I studied my visitor. I had certainly never seen him before. He was small, as I have said, and ugly. And I noticed that being near him gave me a very strong feeling of dislike and sickness. His clothes were very well made, of the best materials, but of a size to fit a much bigger man. That should have amused me, but the distaste that I felt was too strong for amusement.

He was anxious and excited at the same time. "Have you got it?" he cried. "Have you got it?" He was so anxious that he even put his hand on my arm, wanting to shake me. I brushed it off, feeling a strong sense of hatred.

"You forget, sir," I said, "that we have not met each other in the usual way. Please sit down."

"I am very sorry, Dr Lanyon," he said, sitting down. "You are quite right. My anxiety made me forget my manners. I was sent here by your friend Dr Henry Jekyll on an important piece of business. And I believe – a drawer..." He was clearly trying to control himself.

I pointed to the drawer. "There it is, sir," I said.

He jumped out of his seat, and almost ran to it. Then he stopped suddenly and put his hand over his heart. His face was white, and so terrible to see that I was afraid for his life and his mind.

"You must be calm," I said.

He gave me a fearful smile, picked up the drawer, and looked at the things in it. He cried aloud as he saw that they were all there. Then, getting his voice almost under control, he said, "Do you have a measuring glass?"

I gave him what he wanted. He measured some of the liquid from the bottle and added one of the powders. The mixture seemed to boil and give off gases. Then the action stopped, and my visitor put the glass down on the table.

"Lanyon," he said. "You remember the promise you made when you became a doctor of medicine: what happens next is a secret that your promise forces you to keep."

He put the measuring glass to his lips and drank the mixture, all of it. I watched him. With a cry, he took hold of the table, nearly falling. His eyes opened in a stare of shock, and he drew down noisy breaths. Then he seemed to begin to change. He seemed to become bigger. His face went suddenly black, and the parts of it moved and changed. And the next moment I had sprung back against the wall in terror.

"Oh, God!" I heard myself crying again and again.

There, in front of my eyes – pale and shaken, half-unconscious, and reaching out like a man brought back from death – there was Henry Jekyll!

I just cannot write down the things he told me in the next hour. I saw what I saw, I heard what I heard, and my mind and heart were sickened. Now – since he has gone – I ask myself if I believe it, and I can't answer. My life has been shaken to the roots. I can't sleep. Terror is with me every hour of every day and night. I can't think of the evil the man told me about without terrible fear. I think the experience has started me on the road to my

The change from Mr Hyde to Dr Jekyll

death, and I must die soon.   But I will die without know-
ing what to believe about it.   I can only tell you one thing,
Utterson. The creature who came into my house that
night was – as Jekyll himself confessed to me – a man
called Hyde. The police were looking for him everywhere for the murder of Carew.

Hastie Lanyon

Chapter 12
Henry Jekyll's explanation

I, Dr Henry Jekyll, was born in the year 1830. My family was rich. I learnt easily and liked hard work, and I liked to be well thought of by my fellow-men. It seemed certain that I would have an honourable future.

My worst fault was that I loved fun. Many people have found that such a love of fun helps them to enjoy life. But for me it did not fit in with my strong wish to seem serious and to be well thought of. So I hid my pleasures. Even before my education was finished, I was already leading a double life. It was not that my wrongdoing was at all serious, but I could not allow it to appear as a part of my working life.

So, where most people allow others to see them as a mixture of good and bad, there was a deep division in me between the two parts of my nature. I was not dishonest about this. As a doctor I did everything I could to learn more and to help the sick and suffering. The other part of me was just as honest in what it was looking for. But there was great discomfort in the division, in one person, into good and evil. It became clear, in my thinking, that man is not truly one but truly two.

"If," I told myself, "the separate parts could be contained in separate bodies, life would be very much easier. The bad could live in his own bad way, without being annoyed by the other one's wish to appear good. The good could go on his upwards path with no danger of losing his good name through the actions of the other one."

These thoughts suddenly fitted in with some scientific

work I was doing. I found that a certain chemical mixture had the power to make changes to the body to fit the working of the mind. I do not want to be exact about the scientific part of this confession, for two reasons. First, I have learnt that man cannot get rid of the difficulties of this life. If we try to do so, the difficulties come back at us in a new form and in a terrible way. Second, as my story will show, my discoveries were not complete.

I prepared the liquid part of the mixture that my experiments had shown I needed. Then I bought from Maw and Company a great deal of the powder that I had to mix with it. I made the mixture. When the action ended, I drank the liquid that it became.

I felt terrible pain, fearful sickness, and a great shock of the mind. They did not last long. I began to feel better. I felt younger, lighter, freer in my body. My mind was freer too, but it was not the freedom of happy youth. I knew at once that I was evil – ten times as evil. The knowledge delighted me. I was not tied down by the better part of my nature. I stretched out my hands, enjoying the new ease of my movements. And it was then that I saw that I was smaller than before.

I suppose, but I do not know certainly, that this was why Edward Hyde was much smaller and younger than Henry Jekyll: at least nine-tenths of my life had been controlled by the better part of me; the worse part had been much less used, and so it was less tired.

I discovered later that people could not come near me without a feeling of great dislike – they hated me before I had even spoken. I suppose this was because all the people most of us meet are a mixture of good and bad. Nobody had ever met a man like Edward Hyde, who was all bad – all evil.

The next part of my experiment was yet to be tried. I prepared the mixture again and drank it. Once more I suffered the terrible pains of change. The pain ended, and I was again – in nature, size and appearance – Henry Jekyll.

The experiment was a success. I laughed – because Henry Jekyll was not all good; he was the same mixture of good and bad as before. And I decided to use my discovery. I made preparations with great care. As Hyde, I took the house in Soho. As Jekyll, I told my servants that a Mr Hyde – I described him – was to be free to use my house in the square. Then I made the will that you so disliked: if anything happened to me as Dr Jekyll, I could become Edward Hyde without any loss.

The situation seemed perfect. If, as Hyde, I was in trouble, I had only to escape into my workroom through the door in the narrow street. I needed just a moment to mix and drink the liquid, and Edward Hyde disappeared. In his place, sitting quietly at his desk, would be Henry Jekyll, a man nobody could blame.

The pleasures I thought I would find as Edward Hyde were not those of a gentleman, though they were not of the worst kind. But Edward Hyde changed that. His nature being truly evil, the pleasures he looked for were evil. They became worse and worse, cruel and unfeeling.

Chapter 13
Henry Jekyll's explanation ends

As Henry Jekyll, I knew what I had done in the form of Mr Hyde. I thought that his wrongdoing was becoming too evil, and I decided not to bring him back again. I was rather unhappy to lose the feeling of youth, the lightness of step, the excitement of Hyde, but for two months I did not bring him back.

Perhaps it was because he had been kept down for two months that Hyde was so evil when I did make and drink the mixture again. As I drank it, I felt the new power of his cruelty.

That was when the unlucky Sir Danvers Carew asked me a simple question, and I enjoyed striking him again and again. It was not until I had tired myself by my fierce attack that I suddenly felt fear. I ran to my house in Soho and destroyed my papers.

Hyde had a song on his lips and was laughing as he mixed the liquid. The terrible pain of change had hardly ended before Henry Jekyll was on his knees, tears pouring down his face, praying to God to forgive him.

In a way, this action of the Carew murder made my future clear. It was impossible to bring Hyde back into a world that was looking for him to punish his crime with death. I must never use the mixture again. I locked the door from the workroom to the street, and I broke the key.

I decided that I must work harder than ever to help my fellow-men. You know how hard I worked for those who were weak, ill, suffering.

On a fine, clear January day, I was sitting in the sun in

the park, resting after a hard morning's work. My mind was not busy. Perhaps I was sleepily remembering some of the amusements of my youth. Suddenly I had feelings of pain, sickness and shock. When the pain had gone, I looked down. My clothes hung without shape over the smaller body and legs of – Edward Hyde. A moment before, I had been safe, rich, loved. Suddenly I had become a hunted man, homeless, a known murderer.

With the mind of Jekyll, I might have been beaten by this terrible change, which had happened without any warning. Hyde's mind was quick-thinking, and with that power I set myself to look at the situation.

The chemicals I needed to change me back to my form as Dr Jekyll were in the room above my workroom. The workroom door to the street was locked. If I tried to reach the workroom through my house, my own servants would give me to the police. I saw that I must get someone else to go. Lanyon? How could I reach him? If I got safely through the streets, how could I – an unknown and hateful visitor – cause him to go and steal things from his friend Dr Jekyll?

I remembered that one thing was still in Dr Jekyll's form. Even as Hyde, I could still write with my own handwriting. I saw what I must do.

At a cheap hotel in Portland Street I took a room. My clothes made them smile, but the look on my face struck the smile from their lips. They gave me paper, and I wrote two letters, one to Lanyon and one to Poole. I did not trust the hotel servants, so I gave orders that the letters should be registered. That meant that the servant had to bring me a receipt from the post office. The rest of the day was a time of great fear.

When I had returned to my own form at Lanyon's, his

shock certainly hurt me. But what shook me most was the memory of those terrible hours as Hyde. I was filled with fear – not the fear of a murderer's death. It was the fear, the terror of being Hyde that I suffered.

I slept well at home, and in the morning I felt shaken, weakened, but refreshed. I still hated and feared the thought of the beast that slept inside me. But I was once more at home in my own house and near to the chemicals I needed.

I was stepping across the yard to go to my workroom. I was enjoying the cold but clear air when I was struck by the pain and shock that meant a coming change. I had just time to reach my room over the workroom before I was once again attacked by the powerful force of Hyde's evil madness. I had to take double the usual amount of the mixture to get back to my own form and be myself.

Six hours after that, the pain and the change returned, and again I had to take the mixture.

From that day on, it seemed only with great difficulty, and only by immediately taking the mixture, that I was able to look like Jekyll. At all hours of the day and night I would feel the pain and suffer the change. Worst of all, if I slept, or even fell half-asleep for a moment in my chair, it was always as Hyde that I woke up.

I was afraid to sleep. But even when I stayed awake, the change came when the power of the mixture weakened. With my sleeplessness and fear, my health was leaving me. The result was that, as Jekyll weakened, Hyde's power grew.

I cannot go on with this description. No one could believe how much I have suffered. It is my punishment, and it might have continued for years. But a last terrible thing has happened. My supply of the powder that I had bought from Maw and Company was nearly finished. I sent for a new supply and mixed it with the liquid. The usual action followed, but the colour of the mixture was different. I drank it, but nothing happened. Poole will tell you how I have tried every supplier of chemicals in London. I believe now that my first supply of the powder was not pure, and that it was the unknown impurity that gave the mixture its power.

About a week has passed. I am now finishing this explanation after drinking the mixture made with the last of the old powder. This is the last time that Henry Jekyll can think his own thoughts or see his own face (now terribly changed and old) in the glass. And I must bring my confession to an end quickly. If the change comes while I am still writing, Hyde will tear it in pieces. But if some time passes after I have finished it, he will be too busy to destroy it – too busy trying to think of a way to escape the death of a murderer.

Will Hyde be hanged as a murderer? Or will he be brave enough to escape that death by killing himself? I don't know, and I don't care. This is my real hour of death. What comes after will happen to another, not myself. Here, then, I put my pen down and fasten the envelope with my confession in it. And that will bring the life of the unhappy Henry Jekyll to an end.

Questions

Questions on each chapter

1 The door
1. What was Mr Utterson's work?
2. When used Utterson and Enfield to go for a walk together?

2 Mr Enfield's story
1. What did the small man do to the little girl?
2. Who caught and held the small man?
3. Who was the money for?

3 The cheque
1. What do you know (so far in the story) about the man who signed the cheque?
2. What did Mr Utterson know about the cheque?

4 Who is Mr Hyde?
1. Whose will did Utterson read?
2. Who did Utterson go to see?
3. What question did Utterson want to ask?
4. What was the answer to that question?
5. Where was Hyde's house?
6. Where was Henry Jekyll's house?
7. Who did Utterson speak to at Jekyll's house?

5 After dinner
1. Where was the dinner party?
2. What promise did Utterson make after dinner?

6 The Carew murder
1. Where was the young woman?
2. Why could she see the faces of the two men? (Because ...)

3 Why did the girl lose consciousness?
4 Who took a letter to Mr Utterson?
5 What did the police inspector find in the fireplace in Hyde's house?

7 The letter

1 Where was Dr Jekyll when Utterson went to his house?
2 What did Jekyll want Utterson's advice about?
3 Who was the "Member of Parliament"?
4 Who was Mr Guest?
5 What did Guest notice about Hyde's handwriting?

8 Dr Lanyon

1 Why did Utterson go to see Dr Lanyon?
2 What shocked Utterson when he saw Lanyon?
3 What did Utterson ask about in his letter to Jekyll?
4 What happened three weeks after Utterson's visit to Lanyon?
5 What was written on the inside envelope?

9 At the window

1 Where did Utterson and Enfield see Dr Jekyll?
2 Dr Jekyll smiled. And then what happened?

10 The last night

1 Who went to see Mr Utterson?
2 Why did Utterson get his hat and coat?
3 Why did Poole ask Utterson to go quietly?
4 What did Poole want Utterson to hear?
5 What did the note to Maw and Company ask for?
6 Who broke down the door to Jekyll's room?
7 How did Hyde die?
8 What were the three things in the large envelope on the desk?
9 How was Jekyll's will different from his earlier will?
10 Why didn't Utterson send for the police at once?

11 Dr Lanyon's story

1 What did Jekyll's letter ask Lanyon to get?
2 Where was Lanyon to get it from?
3 What did the visitor use for measuring the amount of liquid?

4 What did he do with the mixture?
5 What change did the mixture cause?
6 Who had drunk the mixture before the change?

12 Henry Jekyll's explanation

1 Why did Dr Jekyll hide his pleasures?
2 Why did people hate Mr Hyde?
3 What was the second part of Jekyll's experiment?
4 How did Hyde "disappear" if he was in trouble?

13 Henry Jekyll's explanation ends

1 What was impossible after the Carew murder?
2 Where was Jekyll when the unexpected change (to Hyde) first happened?
3 Why couldn't he reach the workroom from the narrow street?
4 Why couldn't he go through his own house?
5 Why did he send the letters by registered post?
6 Which chemical was nearly finished?
7 What did Jekyll do after drinking the last of the old mixture?

Questions on the whole story

These are harder questions. Read the Introduction, and think hard about the questions before you answer them. Some of them ask for your opinion, and there is no fixed answer.

1 Why, in your opinion, did Robert Louis Stevenson bring Mr Enfield into the story?

2 Other people liked Mr Utterson, the lawyer. What reasons do you find in the story for their liking him?

3 Before he experimented with the mixture of chemicals, how was Dr Jekyll (a) like, and (b) unlike, other men?

4 Write very short notes about these people in the story: a Poole; b Police Inspector Newcome; c a young woman servant; d Sir Danvers Carew; e Mr Guest.

5 Can you explain the change in Jekyll's will between Chapter 4 and Chapter 10?

6 When people saw Mr Hyde, they hated him. What reasons do you find for their hatred?

7 Dr Lanyon had a sudden illness from which he died. Can you explain the cause of his illness and death?

8 If you were making a play of this story, would you use one actor to play both parts, Dr Jekyll *and* Mr Hyde, or would you use two actors? Why?

9 What do you think was Stevenson's purpose in writing this story? For example, was it only to amuse the reader?

New words

butler
the chief manservant of a house

chemistry
the science which studies how matter is made up from its parts. For this study, **chemists** use **chemicals** (the liquids, solids etc, that they put together).

clerk
a person who does written work, etc, in an office

client
a person who pays a lawyer for help and advice

confess
say that one has done wrong; a **confession** is saying or writing that one has done wrong

conscious
able to understand what is happening; **unconscious** = having lost consciousness

experiment
a test (as in science) to find out what will happen

lawyer
a person who gives advice about matters of law

registered letter
a letter sent by post for which one pays more than usual for special treatment. The sender gets an official note (**receipt**) from the post office.

rid
get rid of = cause to disappear

safe
a metal cupboard with very strong lock and sides to keep valuable papers, money, etc, in

scorn
having a very low opinion of; **scornful** = showing that one feels a person or thing to be worth nothing

sign (a letter)
write one's name at the end; the name so written is one's **signature**

slope
the way the letters lean (not straight up and down)

will
a paper that a person has signed to show what is to happen to his or her money, house, etc, after his or her death